I Have Not Yet Begun to Fight!

The Story of John Paul Jones: Hero of the American Navy

written and illustrated

by

Ian Cameron

SCOTTISH CHILDREN'S PRESS

Published in 1999 by
SCOTTISH CHILDREN'S PRESS
Unit 14, Leith Walk Business Centre,
130 Leith Walk, Edinburgh EH6 5DT
Tel: 0131 555 5950 • Fax: 0131 555 5018
e-mail: scp@sol.co.uk
http://www.taynet.co.uk/users/scp

text and illustrations © Ian Cameron, 1997

the right of Ian Cameron to be identified as the Author of this
Work has been asserted by him in accordance with the
Copyright, Designs and Patents Act, 1988

ISBN: 1 899827 78 1

British Library Cataloguing in Publication Data
A catalogue record for this book is available from the British Library

Printed and bound by The Cromwell Press, Trowbridge, Wiltshire

Foreword

*Cathy Hurst, Principal Officer,
American Consulate General, Edinburgh*

My work as the Principal Officer at the American Consulate in Scotland has brought me into contact with some very interesting people. I have met politicians and historians, royalty and students, business executives and sports stars, but some of the most interesting people I have come to know have been introduced to me on the pages of this book. When I first came to Scotland it was important to me to know the history of this great nation. Alexander Graham Bell, the inventor of the telephone, was born in Scotland and moved to America. The American industrialist, Andrew Carnegie, returned to his native Scotland often to relieve the tensions of his business. John Muir must have brought his love of the outdoors with him from Scotland to the United States where he founded the National Parks Association. All of these historical figures and many more bind our two nations together.

If any people in history share a common bond, it is the Scots and the Americans. Both have a sure understanding of the rights of men and women to 'life, liberty and the pursuit of happiness', and both can claim the courageous and flamboyant hero of the American navy, John Paul Jones.

John Paul Jones was a Scotsman first, an American last and a pillar of integrity, strength and honour throughout. His tactical genius and perhaps uncanny luck combined to make him one of the most successful military minds in US Naval history. The only officer to be presented with a gold medal by the Continental Congress in 'commemoration of his valour and brilliant service,' he died in a foreign land and in 1913 finally received a proper hero's burial in the chapel of the United States Naval Academy.

Jones undoubtedly inherited from his Scottish roots a strong will and determination to succeed. Born the fifth child of a gardener, near the small village of Kirkbean on the Solway Coast in south-west Scotland, this obscure boy grew up to associate with great men like Thomas Jefferson and Benjamin Franklin. Once, when it looked like defeat was imminent, his immortal words to the captain of an enemy ship exemplified John Paul's attitude towards life, 'I have not yet begun to fight!' He went on to win that battle in the North Sea near Hull on the east coast of England. Thousands watched from land as John Paul gallantly congratulated his beaten foe on a valiant fight.

From birth to childhood, to the adventures on the high seas, the tale is thrilling and unique. Ian Cameron has intertwined the true history of this hero's life with imagination and colour. As you read, you will find what it was like to live in that tumultuous era of war. You can almost see the tall ships bobbing in the water and smell the fresh sea air as John Paul sets sail to fight another battle.

It is important for children, and parents alike, to read about and understand the lives of historic figures like John Paul Jones. I am glad I had the opportunity to meet John Paul Jones, a Scottish-American hero, and I hope you enjoy meeting him, too.

Mr Rob Bodell
Head Teacher
Kirkbean Primary School
Kirkbean
Dumfries

I HAVE NOT YET BEGUN TO FIGHT!
written and illustrated by Ian Cameron

I feel a sense of privilege being Head Teacher of the school attended by one of Scotland's most famous sons – John Paul Jones. His story has humble beginnings but through his unwavering ambition he never lost sight of what he was trying to achieve on land or at sea.

In this book, Ian Cameron has captured the personality of the man. On one hand his drive and determination often make him appear ruthless, but to balance that we see examples of his chivalry and sense of fair play.

This book will appeal to all children with a sense of adventure. Ian Cameron's enthusiasm and respect for his subject shine through as the story unfolds from his formative years in Kirkbean through to his final journey to Annapolis in the United States. There is much that children today can learn from John Paul Jones. With determination and self-discipline, ambitions can be realised and dreams can indeed come true.

Ian Cameron's book successfully presents the life story of a man who forever will establish links between Kirkbean in Dumfries and Galloway and the United States. If it helps children throughout the world learn more about John Paul Jones then he will have done young people a great service.

On 6 July, 1747, another cry joined the squawks of the seagulls sweeping above the Arbigland Estate of William Craik on the Solway coast, south-west Scotland. In the gardener's thatched-roofed cottage a baby boy, the fifth child of John Paul and his wife, Jean, was loudly announcing his arrival to the world. Little did anyone realise then that this boy, also to be named John, was to become famous far beyond the windswept shores of his birthplace.

The news soon reached the small village of Kirkbean two miles away and was the subject of the day's conversation.

'It's just as well it's a stone building or it would be bursting at the seams. Seven people in a two-roomed cottage is a tight fit.'

'Aye, and only one room for a bedroom – the other being the kitchen with its open fireplace – just as well they have a loft for the youngsters to sleep in during the summer.'

'Winter's different, I know they sleep downstairs on straw-filled hessian sacks to keep warm.'

'Once the new laddie gets his lungs full of some good Scottish sea air he'll do fine.'

John Paul spent his childhood playing by the sea shore and watching the many ships sailing in and out of the Solway Firth. Sometimes he would watch goods, such as tobacco, being unloaded at the nearby port of Carsethorn to be taken by road to Dumfries. Although he enjoyed his time at Kirkbean school, his thoughts were never far from the sea.

'What would you like to do when you leave school?' the teacher asked.

'I want to go to sea. I want to sail on deep water; I want to feel the heave of the deck beneath me.'

By the time John Paul was twelve years old his dreams were to come true. John Younger, a shipowner in the Port of Whitehaven in Cumberland, England, had heard of young John Paul while visiting Kirkcudbright harbour. He looked for the boy and offered him an apprenticeship. John Paul was delighted! He accepted the job and with his family's blessings he sailed the short distance across the Solway Firth to Whitehaven.

Very soon John Paul was on his first voyage as a cabin

boy on the merchant ship, *Friendship*, sailing to Virginia in the American colonies.

'Well, John me lad, it's time to learn the ropes while you're on board,' the mate said and started to teach the eager youngster how to keep a ship in fine trim. By the

time they reached the American coast, John Paul had scaled the rigging, helped pull and set the sails, been taught how to reef, to splice and to steer, and lots of other things a seaman had to know.

'What will you do while we are in port in Virginia?' the captain asked John Paul.

'I'll go and visit my older brother William,' John Paul replied, 'he's a tailor in Fredericksburg.'

His brother was glad to see him. 'Hello, John! What would you like to do to pass the time?'

'I'd like to study navigation,' John Paul said, thinking how useful it would be in his sea-going career.

The fact that he had worked hard while he had been at school helped him with his new studies, and although John Paul missed his family and his three sisters who spoiled him, he was glad to be with his brother who encouraged him to take an interest in literature and the arts.

Sailing across the Atlantic could be very hard and even dangerous, with poor food, tainted water and rough seas, but John Paul loved the life. So he was very disappointed when the Friendship returned to Whitehaven after one of its many voyages and he was told that the business problems of John Younger meant that his apprenticeship had to be cancelled. John Paul was afraid that being only seventeen, he was too young to get another position on a ship. But his sea skills had been noticed by other shipowners and he was appointed as third mate on the Whitehaven ship King George.

John Paul's happiness at being back at sea was short-lived. His new ship's main business was transporting slaves between the West Indies and the American colonies.

'I hate this disgusting trade,' he thought to himself.

When he was nineteen, he transferred to another ship, the Jamaican *Two Friends*, as first mate. This ship was also a 'slaver', but John Paul hoped that his experience in a promoted position would help his job chances on other ships with different cargo. The *Two Friends* was a brigantine – a two-masted vessel with a square rigged foremast and fore-and-aft rigged mainmast, and was a good test of his seamanship in heavy seas.

Eventually, John Paul had enough of the 'disgusting trade' and decided to sail back to Scotland. Booking a passage on the merchantman, *John* of Kirkcudbright, John Paul looked forward to a relaxing journey home. However, when both the captain and the chief mate died of fever, the crew turned to John Paul for help.

'Mr Paul, take command of the vessel. You can steer us safely to our home port,' they said, promising to support him all the way.

John Paul had no choice. 'Aye, I'll do that as I have a wish to reach dry land myself,' he said. Secretly, he was looking forward to proving his seamanship. Once the *John* had reached Scotland, the owners, Currie, Beck & Co., asked John Paul to visit their office.

'We would like to thank you, Mr Paul, for what you have done for us,' they said. 'How would you like to become the master of the *John* and share in the trading profits?'

'I would be honoured, Sirs,' John Paul answered, delighted at the offer. He had become a captain at the age of twenty-one.

Although he was small in height, being only five foot six inches, John Paul had the grit and determination of a Scots terrier and did not suffer fools gladly. He took a great pride in his appearance and because he was quite well educated and good at making conversation he was invited to many dinner parties.

Trading to the West Indies from Britain could mean being away from home for more than a year and this often led to problems with the crew. Masters sometimes had to impose harsh discipline to keep the ship running smoothly.

On his second voyage in charge of the *John*, John Paul had to exert his authority when his ship was in the Port of Tobago.

'Murdo Maxwell, I find you guilty of being lazy and neglecting your duties as ship's carpenter, and I therefore sentence you to be flogged,' he declared before the ship's crew.

After the flogging, Maxwell complained to anyone in Tobago who would listen and then he deserted to join another ship. Shortly afterwards he died at sea.

When the *John* arrived back in Scotland in November 1770, John Paul was surprised to find himself arrested and imprisoned in the Tollbooth of Kirkcudbright.

Maxwell's father, an important man in the town, had charged John Paul with his son's murder. He claimed that the flogging had left his son badly wounded and had led to his death. Despite protests from Maxwell, John Paul was released on bail and he managed to gather enough evidence to prove his innocence.

Currie, Beck & Co. closed down in 1771 and John Paul was given command of a ship trading with the Isle of Man. Soon afterwards he was made master and part owner of the *Betsy* of London, which had commercial business in the West Indies. John Paul began to make a lot of money from trading deals and was living quite a comfortable life when what he was to call 'the great misfortune' happened.

In December 1773, in Tobago, his crew mutinied. Stepping out into the companion-way of the *Betsy*, John Paul met the crew. 'We want our money!' shouted one of the leaders.

'You well know the articles you signed. You'll get your pay when you return to home port. I order you to go forward.' John Paul kept his voice calm as he watched the men in front of him.

'We've been gone from our home port for more than a year now!' they protested. We want to go ashore tonight with money in our pockets!'

'There's money in your cabin!' said another leader, rushing forward. 'Step aside!'

Unfortunately, the crush of the men behind him pushed the man on to the sword John Paul held in his hand and he was killed. It was an accident, but John Paul knew that the crew would be hostile witnesses in any enquiry, and so he asked some of his friends on shore for advice.

'You are in trouble Captain Paul; grave trouble,' said the Lieutenant Governor of the Colony. 'A man was killed aboard your ship . . . and you killed him!'

'It was mutiny and self-defence. It was either kill, or be killed,' John Paul protested.

'Nevertheless, a man has been killed in this harbour and, as in all His Majesty's colonies, that means there must be a trial.'

'I am ready to stand trial any time, Sir,' John Paul said, holding his head high, but the Lieutenant Governor continued.

'It's not that simple. The charge is murder, and that means no bail is allowed. You would be placed in jail to await the pleasure of an Admiralty Court, which might not be held for a year, or two. In the meantime, what becomes of discipline on other ships?'

'I would say it would suffer, Sir . . . if any rascal knows that a Ship's Master rots in jail just for upholding authority,' John Paul answered. 'What do you advise I should do?'

There was silence for a moment.

'Get away from here as fast as you can and stay away until I send for you. When the Admiralty Court calls your case, you will hear from me.'

John Paul took this advice. He arranged for his business interests to be wound up by Mr Ferguson, one of his agents, and he set out for Fredericksburg, Virginia, to visit his brother.

There were more problems waiting for John Paul in the American colony. William had died, and John Paul had to settle his estate. This was a very frustrating time in John Paul's life. He had very little money, as Mr Ferguson in Tobago was slow in his dealings but, worse than that, he was a sailor in a new country without a ship. One of the things he did do at this time was add 'Jones' to his baptismal name.

In American colonies at this time there was talk of revolution against Britain and when the fighting did start at Lexington, Massachusetts, on 19 April 1775, John Paul Jones was unemployed and living on the generosity of strangers. Realising his sea skills would be useful to the new Continental Congress in Philadelphia, John made contact with two influential members of the Congress – Joseph Hewes of North Carolina, and Robert Morris of Pensylvannia. These two men were on the Board set up to organise a Continental Navy. Paul Jones was asked to supervise the fitting out – the making ready for sea – of the *Alfred*, which was berthed in

Philadelphia. It was the first naval ship procured by Congress.

By the time the *Alfred* was ready to sail, it had been joined by another man-of-war, the *Columbas*; two brigantines, the *Cabot* and the *Andrew Doria*; and a sloop, the *Providence* – a small, one-masted, fore-and-aft rigged vessel which only had guns on its upper deck.

The command of the *Alfred* was given to Captain Saltonstall, a man with political friends but little sea experience. When Congressman Hewes told Paul Jones how he had tried at the Marine Committee to gain him the command, he explained, 'Many petitioners . . . and many relatives!'

'The Committee may find that salt-water is thicker than blood. An officer's corps must be built upon training and merit,' Paul Jones replied.

In December that same year, John Paul Jones, being the senior officer on board, was given the honour of being the first person to raise the Grand Union flag, the new flag of the Continental Navy. This flag, which used thirteen alternate red-and-white stripes plus part of the symbol from the British national ensign, flew from the top mast of the *Alfred* on the instructions of Commodore Hopkins.

After the ceremony the Commodore said, 'The ship is commissioned but, allow me to ask, where is the Captain?'

On being told that Captain Saltonstall had sent word that he would be detained for a few more days, Commodore Hopkins said angrily, 'There's your political influence for you! A Captain absent from his ship on such an occasion! How do you expect to make a navy with such?'

He turned to Paul Jones and said, 'I know that you, Sir, will be commissioned Senior Lieutenant by Congress; as of now, I appoint you Captain of this ship.'

The promotion did not last long. A few days later, after last-minute checks and just when the *Alfred* was ready for sea, the tardy Captain Saltonstall appeared and took command.

On the first voyage of the Commodore's small squadron, in March 1776, Paul Jones quickly demonstrated his sea skills and his knowledge of the waters of the American coast. As the fleet sat off the coast of New Providence Island in the Bahamas, a meeting was held on board the *Alfred* – Commodore Hopkins' flagship – to discuss tactics on how to attack the British-held forts. Hopkins outlined the situation as he saw it.

'As every shore battery at Fort Nassau will be pointed at the fleet, the only alternative is to sail round the island and try to land on the other side.' He asked the officers if they had any questions. Not wishing to disagree with their Commodore, all the officers kept quiet. All except Paul Jones.

'Two points, Sir. First, there is no anchorage on the other side of the island; and second, a landing party would have to march across the whole breadth of the island to attack the Fort. Since Fort Nassau expects us – why not attack Fort Montague? Then we could march three miles and take Nassau from the rear.'

The officers immediately protested saying that it could not be done as there were dangerous off-shore reefs.

'We have captured a Nassau pilot who can guide us through the reefs,' explained Paul Jones, 'and we can anchor off Fort Montague, out of gun range. Then, if you give me two hundred marines, we can land in small boats through the surf.'

'Whoever heard of sending marines from a ship to fight on land?' asked the startled Commodore.

'The Vikings, Commodore, a thousand years ago.'

Commodore Hopkins thought for a moment, looked at Paul Jones and said, 'Your audacity amazes me, but somehow you have persuaded me.' Turning to the other officers he said, 'Gentlemen, we will adopt Mr Jones's plan! The conference is over.'

The American fleet was safely guided through the reefs and soon the longboats of the American marines were fanning out in what was to become a pattern for ship-to-shore landings. Not many hours after the Continental leathernecks (they had this nickname because of the high leather collars on their tunics), had splashed ashore, the Grand Union flag was flying over Fort Montague and Fort Nassau. This was a great victory. As well as the two forts, they had also captured a large quantity of arms and ammunition. Paul Jones's reputation was established.

The return cruise was a different story. By the time they sailed into the range of the British man-of-war *Glasgow* off Black Island, the squadron had already captured some small craft off the Bahamas; a six-gun schooner, the *Hawk*; and an eight-gun, two-howitzer bomb brig, called the *Bolton*, off the American mainland. Despite distinguishing himself in charge of the *Alfred's* main gun battery, Paul Jones was dismayed that the inconclusive sea battle ended with the *Glasgow* escaping from the whole American fleet. As a result, two captains were tried in a court-martial and the Captain of the sloop the *Providence* was found guilty of cowardice.

Paul Jones wasn't to blame for the shambles and he was ordered to take command of the *Providence* in May 1776. In August he received his Captain's commission from the President of Congress. A small fleet was put in his charge and he embarked on a series of voyages which were to enhance his reputation for seamanship and tactical ability that was second to none in the American navy.

He sailed from the Delaware Capes under orders to cruise as long as his provisions and water lasted. Addressing the seventy-man crew of the *Providence* he said excitedly, 'The whole Atlantic seaboard is to be our bailiwick. We have the chance to pick up prizes galore from Nova Scotia to the West Indies!'

One of the crew shouted, 'We are small, Sir – and we only carry twelve four-pounder guns.'

'Yes, but we're trim and fast! We will dance through a line of frigates like a French ballerina!' Paul Jones replied with enthusiasm.

The first cruise with Paul Jones as master of the *Providence* was to create havoc for the British navy.

He outwitted two British frigates – the *Solebay* and the *Milford* – and burned and sank six schooners, a ship and a brigantine. He also captured and sent in as prizes six brigantines, a ship and a sloop. The fisheries at Canso and Isle Madame were destroyed and many ships were cut away from their berths.

By the time Paul Jones sailed the *Providence* safely into Rhode Island in October 1776, he was greeted as a hero. In November he and his entire crew were transferred to the *Alfred* and they set sail for Nova Scotia. Accompanying them was the *Providence,* now under the captainship of Hoysteed Hacker.

Off Louisburg they captured a merchant ship, then they found a major prize – the *Mellish* – a transport ship which was laden with a valuable cargo of soldiers' clothing.

A few days later the *Alfred* lost contact with *Providence* in a light gale. Hacker used this as an excuse to return to port and claim many of their successes for himself.

Paul Jones carried on alone and burned a large ship off Canso as well as the on-shore oil warehouses. He cut three ships out from under the nose of the British frigate, the *Flora*, off Cape Breton. On his way home, he fooled the *Milford* for a second time, much to the delight of his crew, and in December sailed into Boston harbour with his prizes.

He was completing his list of all the ammunition, medical supplies and surgical instruments which he had prevented from reaching the British General Burgoyne's Army when he received some devastating news from Congressman Hewes.

'You are no longer in command,' he said. 'While you were at sea, the Marine Committee compiled a naval list for Congress which determined the rank of the naval captains. You have been placed eighteenth on the seniority list, behind many captains who entered the service after you – I am sorry.'

Paul Jones was shocked into silence for a moment and then he said, 'A thousand useful things we can learn from the King's navy. Instead, we adopt its worst fault: appointment by political or family influence! This must be stamped out or we'll have no navy!'

Many efforts were made to place Paul Jones higher on the list and gain him a ship, but all without success. One excuse was that he was a newcomer in America and, even worse, British.

'I am a Scot!' argued Paul Jones. 'No Scot is a stranger to the cause of freedom!'

The fact that he did not hide his contempt for some of the Northern naval officers and that he had entered the navy from the South did not help his cause. There still existed some distrust and bad feeling between the North and South, and the Northern colonies regarded Southerners – and therefore John Paul Jones – as 'Johnny-come-latelys'.

Eventually Congress realised they could not do without his skills and issued the statement:

In Congress, June 14, 1777

First: Resolved that the flag of the United States be thirteen stripes, alternate red and white; that the Union be thirteen stars, white, in a blue field, representing a new constellation;

Second: Resolved that Capt. J. Paul Jones be appointed to command the *Ranger*.

Once again John Paul Jones was the first person to raise a new flag when he flew the 'Stars and Stripes' on the masthead of the sloop, the *Ranger*. With his usual attention to detail, Paul Jones supervised the outfitting and manning of his ship but this took longer than expected and he did not sail from Portsmouth, New Hampshire, until 1 November 1777.

Congress ordered him to sail to France and report to the American commissioners in Paris. He was to give them the news that in October General Burgoyne had surrendered to the American Army, commanded by

General Gates, at Saratoga on the Hudson river. He was also promised that he would be given command of the *Indien*, a new frigate which Congress was having built in Amsterdam.

On the voyage across the Atlantic, John Paul Jones was in good spirits; the *Ranger* was handling well in deep water and he would soon be standing on the deck of a large frigate. He was also pleased by the fact that he would soon escape from the interference of politicians and political captains.

When he reached Nantes, he discovered that the news of Burgoyne's capitulation had arrived before him. His disappointment was increased when he was told in Paris that the *Indien* had been sold to the French by the resident American commissioners for political reasons.

Paul Jones felt frustrated, angry and betrayed because he had already written to Congress stating that his 'heart's first and favourite wish was to be employed in active and enterprising services' and that the honour done him by the Congress caused him to be full of 'sentiments of gratitude which I shall carry with me to my grave'.

He felt he had made a fool of himself and that others were making a fool of him.

The American commissioners in France at that time were Benjamin Franklin, Silas Deane and Arthur Lee. Paul Jones did not hesitate to tell them what he thought.

'Gentlemen, I did not come here to study politics – I came here to fight!'

Franklin urged him to be patient and to make himself at home as his guest in Paris. Paul Jones was young and good-looking, although well under six feet, and was quickly welcomed into Parisian society. He moved around the capital being witty and charming; entertaining the ladies in the evening so that during the day he could be clever and serious with their husbands – hoping to find a suitable command.

In mid January 1778 Benjamin Franklin asked Paul Jones what he would like to do with the *Ranger*. The answer was swift and to the point.

'Sir, I intend to invade the British Isles!' When questioned on his statement Paul Jones explained, 'A landing on the English coast, no matter how small, would shake the gentlemen in Whitehall as nothing has yet. It would be so unexpected.'

Seeing the interest in Franklin's face, Paul Jones continued. 'British navy ships would have to be diverted to home waters – popular opinion would mount against the war. Many an Englishman is against it, anyhow!'

Franklin was so impressed that he issued orders, counter-signed by Deane, that Paul Jones should make ready the *Ranger* and, 'proceed with her . . . distressing the enemies of the United States.'

Arthur Lee did not sign the orders as he was not happy

with the way it was proposed to distribute any prizes from the venture.

Paul Jones spent several weeks on the *Ranger* cleaning and caulking the hull and checking the mainmast which had been restepped, or moved, farther aft in an effort to reduce the strain on the ship during bad weather. Food and water were stored in the hold, and gunpowder and shot was loaded into the magazine deep in the bowels of the ship.

With a newly rigged ship and a crew which had just been paid, the *Ranger* sailed north to Brest. On the way,

passing the French fleet in Quiberon Bay, Paul Jones acknowledged the French Admiral with a thirteen-gun salute which was returned with a nine-gun reply. This was the first time the 'Stars and Stripes' had been recognised by a European country.

Paul Jones sea tested the *Ranger* in foul weather in the Bay of Biscay and off the Brittany coast, and found that more work needed to be done on the ship. Putting into Brest, the *Ranger* had her masts taken out and completely restepped, new sails were cut and others altered and the ballast was shifted to improve the trim.

While this work was being done, Franklin, Deane and Lee were officially received by King Louis XVI and Queen Marie Antoinette, and on 7 April an order came from Versailles that all American warships were to be welcomed and assisted in French ports.

A few days later the *Ranger* left port escorted by the French frigate, the *Fortunee*, and its tender of accompanying smaller vessels whose mission was to make sure the *Ranger* got safely past the British patrols.

Soon the *Ranger* was on its own, facing and sinking a brigantine and taking its crew on board as prisoners. On 17 April Paul Jones sunk a large merchant ship, the *Lord Chatham*, in the St George's Channel between England and Ireland after which the *Ranger* continued to sail north.

There were other successes but sometimes the weather was so stormy and severe that Paul Jones had to shelter along the south shore of Scotland. However, by 22 April the weather and visibility at sea had improved so much that Paul Jones remarked to his officers, 'Look about you, gentlemen, as far as the eye can see there are three kingdoms covered with snow.'

That evening he called a conference in his cabin. 'Gentlemen,' he addressed his officers. 'That land looming off our bows is the port of Whitehaven, the port from which I first set sail as a cabin boy. During the night I plan to enter the harbours and burn all the shipping we find.'

One startled officer asked, 'It will surely be fortified, won't it, Sir?'

'Correct! There are two forts which I intend to capture with two boatloads of men before dawn. Any comments?'

Another officer, who could not see any profit in the venture, muttered, 'If we're caught we'll be hanged as pirates!'

Paul Jones looked him in the eye and said, 'My plan is that we will not be caught, Mr Simpson. You, Sir, will take one boat into the inner harbour. I, myself, will take the landing party ashore to attack the other fort.'

Before dawn the daring plan was put into effect. Quietly, Paul Jones and his party crept to the main guardroom of the forts. Outside the door, he whispered to his men, 'Now we strike a blow for freedom, lads!'

'Aye, Sir,' a marine replied, 'and quite a blow it'll be to those Tories!'

Bursting the guardroom door open, Paul Jones shouted to the startled British soldiers inside. 'I am Captain John Paul Jones of the American Continental Navy and you are my prisoners. Make no disturbance and you'll be all right! If you move, it will be at your own risk!'

The surprise tactics worked. The British troops were rounded up, the thirty-six guns in the forts were spiked and the signal was given to set the shipping on fire.

Unfortunately, Lieutenant Simpson, who had little faith in the plan, had taken his men on shore to one of the taverns which were open all night. Their presence in the town raised the alarm and the two American boats had to flee back to the *Ranger*, leaving the shipping in both harbours undamaged apart for one small fire.

At noon the same day Paul Jones landed on St Mary's Isle, a wooded peninsula near Kirkcudbright which was the home of the Earl of Selkirk. Paul Jones intended to seize the Earl as a hostage and use him to bargain for better treatment for American prisoners in English jails. When he heard that the Earl was not at home, Paul Jones turned to go back to his ship. But then he had more trouble with Lieutenant Simpson.

'Captain, the men and myself feel we have come a long way for nothing,' said Simpson, blocking the way.

'What are you suggesting, Sir?' asked Paul Jones.

'The house is full of silver,' Simpson said. 'I am suggesting we relieve his Lordship of his plate.'

'We are not common pirates, Sir!' Paul Jones replied angrily.

There was menace in Simpson's voice when he said, 'No, Sir, neither are we common mutineers.'

Sensing the mood of discontent among the landing party, Paul Jones reluctantly agreed to their demands, with conditions. 'Very well, Sir, but you will take Lieutenant Wallingford with you; the crew stays outside and the household will come to no harm – do I make myself clear?'

The silver was taken, the Countess of Selkirk, her family and servants were treated with chivalry and an embarrassed Paul Jones quickly sent a letter promising to return the goods after the war.

The next day, off Carrickfergus on the Irish coast, the *Ranger* faced up to the British ship of war, *HMS Drake*. The Captain of the *Drake* had heard about the raid on Whitehaven and displayed caution at first before calling through a megaphone to Paul Jones to identify himself.

Paul Jones answered with pride, 'The American

Continental ship, the *Ranger* – we are waiting for you; please to come on!'

In just over an hour, the *Drake's* captain was dead, his second officer mortally wounded, and the third officer had surrendered. Paul Jones lost eight men – crewmen who had been killed or wounded – and the *Drake* lost forty-two.

After this battle almost half of the British navy in home waters went searching for the *Ranger*, but Paul Jones took his ship, the *Drake* and his other prizes round the north of Ireland and back to France.

News of Paul Jones's deeds caused panic in Britain, particularly in England and in government circles. In official circles he was referred to as a pirate or 'corsair', and it was claimed that he fought 'with a halter round his neck' – a reference to his troubles in Tobago. Many people were frightened and angry that Britain had been invaded and John Paul Jones became such a frightening figure that at night mothers told their restless children to 'go to sleep or John Paul Jones will come and get you!'

When the *Ranger* sailed into Brest, after an absence of only twenty-eight days, all France regarded Paul Jones as a hero.

In June, at Versailles, the French marine minister asked if Paul Jones could stay in France to lead a future naval expedition. Although pleased at this prospect, Paul Jones was not happy when he was ordered to hand over the command of the *Ranger* to the treacherous Lieutenant Simpson who later sailed it back to America.

For the rest of 1778 and into early 1779, events involving politics, diplomacy and personal grudges meant that Paul Jones was an unhappy, unemployed and frustrated captain looking for a command. Benjamin Franklin suggested he look at captured ships which could be turned into warships, but at first nothing seemed suitable. There were ships available but John Paul Jones had a special kind of ship in mind. In a letter to Franklin he wrote, 'I wish to have no connection with any ship that does not sail fast, for I intend to go IN HARM'S WAY.'

Finally, he saw an old East Indiaman, the *Duc de Duras*, which needed a lot of work but could get him back to sea.

When asked what name he had for the ship, Paul Jones replied, 'I would like to honour my dear friend, Benjamin Franklin. I never sail without his book, *Poor Richard*. I should like to give that name to my ship . . . What would *Poor Richard* be in French?' he asked, and on being told said, 'Then *Bon Homme Richard* it will be.'

Paul Jones supervised the conversion of his vessel into

a warship which mounted twenty-eight twelve-pounders on the gun deck, six nine-pounders on the forecastle and six eighteen-pounders in the gunroom below the main battery. The eighteen-pounders, although they appeared formidable, were rarely used as they were mounted so low and their gun ports had to be kept closed in heavy seas.

Plans were made by the French government and the American commissioners for Paul Jones to be the commodore of a naval squadron which was also to carry seven hundred French troops commanded by General Lafayette.

For political reasons this plan was abandoned and on 14 August five naval vessels and several privateers sailed from L'Orient with marines but no solders on board. Apart from the *Bon Homme Richard*, the squadron, proudly flying the 'Stars and Stripes,' included the thirty-six gun *Alliance*, the thirty-gun *Pallas*, the eighteen-gun *Cerf* and the twelve-gun *Vengeance*.

Sailing round Ireland and the north of Scotland, many prizes were taken but Paul Jones had constant trouble with Peter Landais, the French Captain of the *Alliance*.

The news of Paul Jones's approach down the east coast of Scotland caused panic in Edinburgh. Fear spread as the *Bon Homme Richard* sailed into Leith harbour on 16 September. However, stormy weather saved Leith, and then Kirkcaldy, from planned raids. At least one Scottish

minister was convinced God had responded to the prayers of the people and had produced winds strong enough to blow Paul Jones out of the Firth of Forth.

On 23 September the *Bon Homme Richard* and the two ships that had kept up with it, the *Alliance* and the *Pallas*, intercepted the forty-one vessel, Baltic merchant fleet. It was protected by two impressive warships – the forty-four gun *Serapis* and the twenty-gun *Countess of Scarborough*.

The merchant ships were sent towards the River Humber for safety and under a full harvest moon the warships faced up to each other off the Yorkshire coast near Flamborough Head. Paul Jones knew that the *Serapis* out-classed his ship in gunpower, size and speed, and his only hope of success was to engage in close combat, relying on his musketry.

Displaying skillful seamanship, Paul Jones placed the *Richard* alongside the *Serapis* and lashed the two ships together.

For the next three hours the two vessels pounded each other with every gun available. Savagely, the crews fought hand-to-hand on the decks and in the ships' rigging.

To add to Paul Jones's troubles, Captain Landais in the *Alliance* – who was supposed to be on the American side

– circled round both ships firing at each of them! Both ships were on fire in various places but the *Bon Homme Richard* was so badly damaged that it was slowly sinking.

Noticing this, Captain Pearson of the *Serapis* thought he had won. He used a megaphone to shout above the din, 'Are you surrendering? Do you ask for quarter?'

'No, Sir!' John Paul Jones shouted back. 'I HAVE NOT YET BEGUN TO FIGHT!'

Shortly afterwards, with his masts down, his main battery disabled and several dangerous fires throughout his ship, Captain Pearson struck his colours and the *Serapis* was surrendered.

When Captain Pearson offered his sword, Paul Jones returned it saying, 'You have fought gallantly, Sir, and I hope your King will give you a better ship.'

The *Pallas* had also struck a blow for the American cause by capturing the *Countess of Scarborough*. The battle, which had been watched by thousands of people standing on the Yorkshire shore and cliffs, had been a terrible bloodbath with hundreds killed and wounded on both sides.

Paul Jones transferred his crew to the *Serapis* and, when the *Richard* had sunk, sailed with what was left of his squadron to Texel in Holland where he pressed charges against Landais and took command of the *Alliance*.

Frustrated after months of bitter diplomatic wrangles,

Paul Jones finally set sail from Holland in December. After escaping a British blockading squadron he cruised as far south as Spain looking for prizes before putting into L'Orient in February 1780.

He began to refit the *Alliance* to make ready for his return to America. While he was in L'Orient he took the opportunity to write many letters asking for the money which was due to his crew. For a considerable time, John Paul Jones had been funding his ventures himself, which meant paying his crew out of his own pocket rather than wait for the long overdue payments from the Continental Congress.

In pursuit of this money, Paul Jones went to Paris in April and was very surprised to find himself greeted with applause everywhere he went. He was treated as the popular hero of the American Revolution. Festivals were held in his honour and a bust of him was commissioned from Houdon, a popular sculptor. At Versailles, the Queen presented him with a fob chain and seal while the King gave him a gold-hilted sword and made him a Chevalier of France.

Paul Jones enjoyed the attention and did not return to L'Orient until June. He was too late: the disgraced Landais had taken over the *Alliance* and sailed to America. Finally, in February 1781, Paul Jones reached America in the French ship, the *Ariel,* and in April Congress formally thanked him.

He was elected to command the *America* which was being built in New Hampshire. It was to be a great ship and took over a year to build, but after it was launched it was presented to France. After a few months' experience sailing with the French navy, Paul Jones was asked by Congress to go to Paris in 1783 as agent for prize money. This money was due to America for the prizes taken in European waters by Paul Jones's ships. After six months, an agreement was reached in Paris but the payment was delayed for a considerable time.

Three years later, Paul Jones returned to America and in 1787 Congress presented him with a gold medal in commemoration of his valour and brilliant service. He was the only officer of the Continental Navy to be distinguished in this way. His fame had spread far and wide and later that year he took the advice of Thomas Jefferson, who was the new ambassador to France, and accepted an offer from Catherine the Great to join the Russian navy as Rear Admiral, a far higher rank than he had achieved in the American navy.

Sent to the Black Sea in a campaign against the Turks, Paul Jones (now called Kontradmiral Pavel Ivanovich Jones) distinguished himself only to find his victories were credited to others. In one daring adventure, Paul

Jones rowed out at night through the Turkish fleet noting the details of the assembled enemy ships. Picking out the biggest vessel, he wrote on its side 'to be burned – John Paul Jones'!

Despite his efforts, he was steadily undermined by his enemies (some of them very powerful like the French adventurer Prince Nassau-Siegen, and Admiral Prince Potemkin) and the only award he received was the decoration of the cross of the Order of St Anne – poor recognition of his naval feats.

While on leave in St Petersburg in March 1789 he was falsely accused of molesting a young girl. He appealed to the Empress Catherine and after some difficulty was given his back pay and sent on two years' leave. He returned to Paris feeling very bitter. His health had suffered and, shortly after making out his will, John Paul Jones died alone on July 1792. He was 45 years old.

His body was wrapped in a plain white shroud, without any uniform or medals, and was sealed in a lead coffin which was filled with alcohol. He was buried in an unmarked grave. His body lay in St Louis Cemetery for Protestants outside Paris for more than a hundred years until President Theodore Roosevelt ordered that it be taken to America.

Accorded all the honours of a great national hero, the United States Navy provided an escort of warships to carry the body of John Paul Jones back to the land of his adoption. In 1913 his body was finally laid to rest in a marble sarcophagus in the chapel at the United States Naval Academy in Annapolis.

John Paul Jones – Hero or Villain?

A father of the United States Navy and a Famous Scot. Certainly, John Paul Jones was a man who kept his promises. In 1789 he bought, with his own money, all the silver plate that had been taken on the raid at St Mary's Isle. He returned the family silver and in a letter to the Countess of Selkirk he described himself as 'A citizen of the world, totally unfettered by the little, the mean distinctions of climate and country, which diminish the benevolence of the heart and set bounds to humanity.'

Selected titles from Scottish Children's Press

Columba
Bernard MacLaverty
ISBN: 1 899827 46 3   Ages 9+   £2.99
An audio tape of this book is also available, priced £2.99
Columba Book and Tape Pack
ISBN: 1 899827 75 7   Ages 9+   £4.99

The Crown Jewels of Scotland
Moira Small
ISBN: 1 899827 35 8   Ages 5+   £2.99
An audio tape of this book is also available, priced £2.99
The Crown Jewels of Scotland Book and Tape Pack
ISBN: 1 899827 82 X   Ages 9+   £4.99

Discover Scotland's History
A. D. Cameron
ISBN: 1 898218 76 5   All Ages   £12.99

Scotland in Roman Times
Antony Kamm
ISBN: 1 899827 14 5   Ages 8+   £4.95

Wallace, Bruce, and the War of Independence
Antony Kamm
ISBN: 1 899827 15 3   Ages 8+   £4.95

these are just some of our history titles – for details on our children's cookery, poetry, fiction, Scots, and early reader books, please contact us for a free catalogue